# The Littlest Coyote Christmas

## by NM Reed
## &
## McCarthy Preston

**Illustrations by:**

**JD Soriano**
**&**
**NM Reed**

# The Littlest Coyote Christmas

# The Littlest Coyote Christmas

## Reviews:

1. Young girls and boys would surely love this book! Among other things, it teaches them that it's okay to make mistakes and that family will still accept them no matter what. *-Lily Garcia, Journalist*
2. I give *The Littlest Coyote Christmas* 5 stars! It is cleverly written. The beautifully illustrated scenes caught my eye and made the story more amusing. My little kid will surely love this read. *-Billy Jay Manguera, Finance Supervisor*
3. I would greatly recommend this book to readers aged 3-9. This is the kind of story I would have loved to read when I was younger. It gives me a sense of comfort even to me as an adult reader and I enjoyed it a lot! *-John Lexus, Legal Assistant*
4. This story is beautifully heartwarming and Littlest Coyote is a character that represents every kid. It surely will be a staple bedtime Christmas story for all the kids out there.*-Sherwin James, Civil Engineer*
5. A beautiful story with remarkable illustrations that will enchant small children with lessons about the importance of love in the season of Christmas. *DD Albert, HR Manager*
6. Lightly rhyming texts encourage fun reading and provide snugly comfort to the readers. I love how it shows the perspective of a pet while teaching kids the essence of love, family, and friendship. *-Mary Anne David, Librarian*
7. This stunningly presented book takes you on a coyote's Christmas adventure with his family. Once you start reading The Littlest Coyote Christmas, you cannot put down this impressive read. *-Julie Bishop, Book Critic*
8. Written in rollicking rhyme, every page of this book features illustrations that will surely amuse youngsters. A must-read! *-Veronica Cruz, Online ESL Instructor*
9. This amazing book contains every bit of what a kid wants in a storybook; a relatable character, pets, friendships, family, and, of course, gorgeous prints. Highly recommended for kids and kids at heart. *-Bella Davis, Technical Writer*
10. As an educator, I am in love with how it is written. Each page features rhymes and alliterations, making it perfect for early childhood and kids learning to read. *-Claudeene Alonzo, Kindergarten teacher*
11. I really enjoyed *The Littlest Coyote Christmas,* even as an adult. It is amazingly written and shows the comfort a family can provide to young kids, even to pets. I enjoyed following LilCoy's adventures and how his Christmas ended the way it should be. *-Mimie Gilbuela, Journalist and Voice-over Artist*

The year was growing old, the weather getting cold,
and the Littlest Coyote was inside.
Outside sat his friends, and snow was on the wind.
But his joy he could not hide.

1

Christmas time had come, the family to be not out-done,
with shining decorations all around.
And Coyote felt the part, he felt it in his heart, Love and
Joy were abound.

He acted out at that, barked at the cat, and pulled the blankets to the ground.

But never did he see, something quite as lovely, as
the blinking, shining Christmas tree.

4

The lights switched on and what a display!
Coyote couldn't wait to play.

"Oh, no!' cried the cat. "Don't you dare do that!"
But it was too late and Coyote ruined the day.

His legs got caught in a tangled knot, and he fell with the
tree right on top.
And tangled on the floor, he lay.

At the sound of the crash, his family came running.
And the cats stood and looked disapproving.
Coyote crawled under the couch barely moving.

There was shouting and running, and poor Coyote was hiding. Someone pulled him out from there.

The front door slammed and Coyote was jammed outside in the cold, cold air.

For a long time, the three dogs stood and stared out in the cold, cold air.

The door never opened like they'd been hopin', and their hearts felt entirely bared.

The door finally opened and the family appeared,
their arms are loaded with bright shiny things.

They all got in the car, saw there were stars and
drove off in the dark evening.

As they drove along through the snow, the Littlest
Coyote thought slow,

"A Ride in the car! I hope we go far! I wonder how
far we will go!"

The family sings songs as they trundle along,
Coyote's head out the window.

He sniffed and he sniffed as the wind blew his
mane, his tongue hanging out there below.

They drove for a while, Coyote had a smile.

Then they stopped at a big gray building, parking. "Couldn't be too bad," thought Coyote. He could hear dogs barking.

But his little girl was crying, so tight she was trying
to hold Coyote secure.

The car door opened, but Coyote cowered away,
inside the warm car he wanted to stay.

But the man picked him up and carried him away.

The Littlest Coyote was afraid and he couldn't stop shaking.

In a cage in a room he sat alone quaking.

He could hear the family's car as it drove away and left him there in that strange cold place.

He heard noises and a bark, and realized he was not alone in the dark.

Other dogs in the dark, at Coyote they barked and he let out a sad coyote howl. Coyote thought back on his day and wondered what he had done so wrong.

He had barked at the cat carefree. Then he'd ruined that beautiful tree. Now his heart was empty of glee.

Late that night to his deathly fright, one of the dogs spoke. "Pssst! Hey kid! Let's have some fun." To the sound Coyote woke. But with all Coyote had been through, his joy was now undone.

"Don't listen to him, dude," the bigger dog said.
"He'll lead you astray!"  The dogs laughed but
Coyote didn't understand and in the back of his cage
he stayed.

The biggest dog spoke, "I'm named Murr. And I'd love to sniff a feast."

The middle dog said, "I am Frankie Frankincense. We come from the east in peace."

Then the caged dogs broke into a sad, sad song:

We three dogs have traveled so far;

We got caught and put behind bars;

Walking, whiffing, ever sniffing,

We three kings we are!

We three Kings from Dog Town we be;

Looking and sniffing at all that we see;

Laws dropped the boom, and sealed our doom,

And put us in a locked dog room.

All night long we whine and bark;

Lights switched off leaves us in the dark.

Dog bowls full of alley cat pee,

Leaves no water for all of us three.


We three dogs of friendship we be;

Wise dogs and kings we are all of us three.

We come with words of comfort and doom

For all of you dogs locked in this room.

Shaking with fear the Littlest Coyote fell asleep. He dreamed of tough guys and fast girls to join in the back street.

But when he awoke in the morning the light streamed in.

A beautiful day was about to begin.

Suddenly, outside he heard a voice and a car. His family had come back for him, they'd traveled so far! The door opened and Coyote barked when the face of his papa appeared in the dark.

The father picked him up from the cage and loaded him in with the family. Maybe they weren't so mad at him, because they loved him anyway!

Grandma was wrinkly but her eyes were twinkly and she pulled a small thing from her sweater.

Coyote ate the bacon because his heart was achin' and he was happy he felt so much better.

The car ride home with grandma and child, Coyote's tongue was trailing. The rest of the car is stuffed with gifts, family love and joy prevailing.

When they arrived home, the house was waiting. The snow
and the lights and the dogs anticipating.

Joy and gifts and family love, and a Christmas tree
to share it.

But this time he vowed to not go near it. But when
he got inside he couldn't bear it.

He walked over to see the Christmas tree displaying. A little blue fence was the family's defense against Coyote's rambunctious playing.

On Christmas morning, with children imploring, they all gathered to the tree beside.

Paper and boxes they tore apart like foxes that were around the presents to hide.

He could stand it no longer; he'd been waiting with wonder, the little brown fence he was outside.

The family cried, "I can't see Coyote! Where did he go? Did he hide?"

The cats could see the Littlest Coyote had jumped
into the pile to hide.

The Littlest Coyote and his doggie friends thank you
for reading their story,

a tale of discovery, redemption, and joy.

No animal actors were harmed in the making of this
book.

And The Littlest Coyote and his family wish your family a very Merry Christmas to all of you and your loved ones!

The Littelst Coyote and his family
say to you and all your loved ones,
Have a Very Merry Christmas

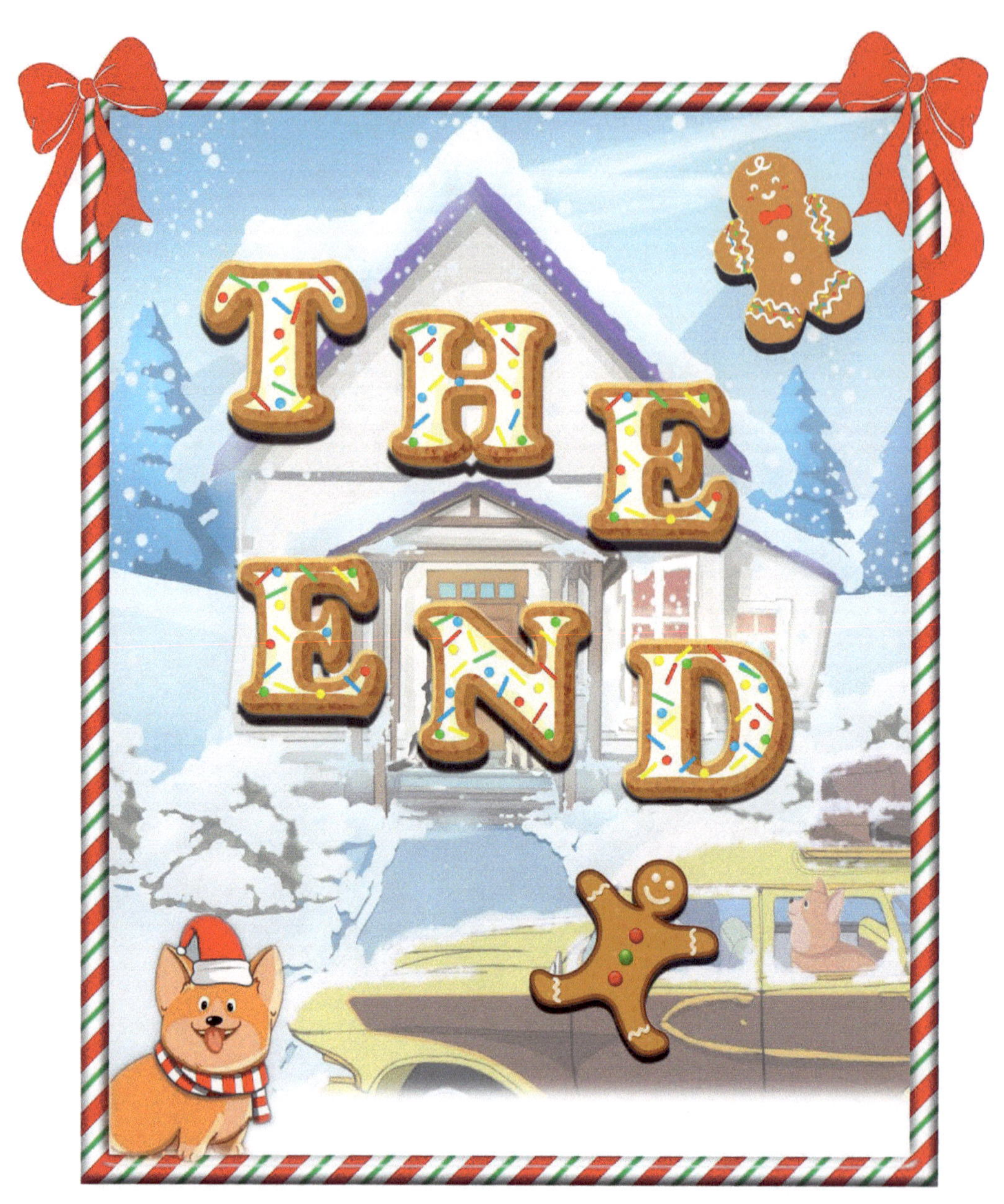

THE
END